JE Reada
cr2

W9-BTP-635
3 5674 03604794 3

DEC - - 2002
LI

THE CLUBHOUSE

A Viking Easy-to-Read

Story by **Anastasia Suen**

Illustrations by **Allan Eitzen**

Based on the characters created by

Ezra Jack Keats

VIKING

VIKING
Published by the Penguin Group
Penguin Putnam Books for Young Readers,
345 Hudson Street, New York, New York 10014, U.S.A.
Penguin Books Ltd, 80 Strand, London WC2R 0RL, England
Penguin Books Australia Ltd, Ringwood, Victoria, Australia
Penguin Books Canada Ltd, 10 Alcorn Avenue, Toronto, Ontario, Canada M4V 3B2
Penguin Books (N.Z.) Ltd, 182-190 Wairau Road, Auckland 10, New Zealand

Penguin Books Ltd, Registered Offices: Harmondsworth, Middlesex, England

First published in 2002 by Viking,
a division of Penguin Putnam Books for Young Readers.

1 3 5 7 9 10 8 6 4 2

Copyright © Ezra Jack Keats Foundation, 2002
Text by Anastasia Suen
Illustrations by Allan Eitzen
All rights reserved

LIBRARY OF CONGRESS CATALOGING-IN-PUBLICATION DATA
Suen, Anastasia.
The clubhouse / by Anastasia Suen ; illustrated by Allan Eitzen.
p. cm.
Based on the characters created by Ezra Jack Keats.
Summary: Peter, Amy, Archie, Lily and Louie work together to build a
clubhouse in a vacant lot.
ISBN 0-670-03537-8
[1. Clubhouses—Fiction. 2. Cooperativeness—Fiction.] I. Keats, Ezra
Jack. II. Eitzen, Allan, ill. III. Title.
PZ7.S94343 Cl 2002
[E]—dc21
2001006527

Viking® and Easy-to-Read® are registered trademarks of Penguin Putnam Inc.

Printed in Hong Kong
Set in Bookman

Reading Level: 1.8

THE CLUBHOUSE

t Bri
gree
e@be
n ch
perks
the re
The We
* Certified, carin
* Pre-school thr
* Small class siz
* Challenging a
* Spanish, art,
arting Oct
AT THE QUA
tion Co
VA Bene

Peter, Amy, Archie, Lily, and Louie

met at Mrs. Lopez's store.

"Where can we play today?" asked Peter.

"My baby sister is asleep," said Lily.

"My aunt is visiting," said Archie.

"My mom works at home today," said Louie.

"They're painting our apartment," said Amy.

"We don't have any place to play," said Lily.

"We can make a clubhouse," said Amy.

"A clubhouse?" said Peter. "Where?"

"Right there," said Lily.

"But how?" said Peter. "All I see is junk."

"My dad says one man's trash

is another man's treasure," said Louie.

"That's right," said Amy. "Look over there."

"Wood!" said Lily. "Let's ask Mrs. Lopez

if we can use it!"

Amy and Lily went into the store.

"What a crazy idea," said Peter.

"You can't build a clubhouse with

that junk," Archie said.

Lily and Amy came out of the store.

"Mrs. Lopez said yes!" said Amy.

"She did?" said Peter.

"Come on," said Amy.

"Okay," said Louie. And he followed the girls.

"We have to move this trash," said Amy.

She rolled a tire out of the way.

Louie dragged a muffler.

Lily picked up newspapers and boxes.

"There's a lot of trash on that lot," said Peter

"That pipe is in the way," said Archie.

"We can move it," said Peter.

Peter and Archie moved the pipe.

"Now we need wood," said Amy.

Amy pulled on a board. It was too heavy.

Lily took the other end. It was still too heavy.

"It looks like they need help," said Archie.

"You need four people to lift that one," Peter said.

"We'll help," said Archie.

One, two, three, four! Up it went!

"Put it here," said Louie.

They put the wood on the ground.

Amy sat on the wood. "It's perfect," she said.

"It's not a clubhouse yet," said Lily.

"It's not?" said Amy.

"Everyone can see you," said Louie. "No walls."

"Oh," said Amy.

"Mrs. Lopez said we could use *all* the wood,"
said Lily.

"So let's get busy," said Peter.

They carried all the wood over.

"Now what?" said Amy.

"Hold this board," said Peter.

"I'll hold the other one," said Archie.

"Now put them together," said Lily.

WHAM! The boards fell down.

"We need nails," Peter said.

"Nails?" said Archie.

"Yes, nails," said Lily, and she pointed to Mr. Frank's hardware store.

"Let's go," said Peter.

"What can I do for you?" asked Mr. Frank.

"We're building a clubhouse," said Archie.

"And we need nails," said Peter.

"I see," said Mr. Frank.

Everyone put money on the counter.

Five nickels, three quarters, and two dimes.

"You have enough for nails," said Mr. Frank.

"But you'll need a hammer, too."

"How much is a hammer?" asked Amy.

"Much more than this," said Mr. Frank.

Mr. Frank looked out the window.

"I made a clubhouse when I was young," he said.

Then he pushed the money away.

"Keep your money," he said. "You can

borrow the hammer and nails."

"Thank you, Mr. Frank!" said the kids.

Peter took the hammer.

Amy scooped up the money.

Then they all went back across the street.

"Here we go," said Lily.

"Hold them tight," said Amy.

Peter hammered in the nails.

BAM! BAM! BAM!

One by one the walls went up.

"Now for the roof," said Louie.

"Here we go," said Peter. "Lift!"

Peter, Amy, Archie, and Lily lifted the last board.

BAM! BAM! BAM! BAM! BAM! BAM!

"Wow!" said Louie.

"We did it," said Lily.

"Let's go inside," said Archie.

"It's perfect," said Peter.

"It's not a clubhouse yet," said Amy.

"It's not?" said Peter.

"We need to have a party!" said Amy.

She emptied her pocket.

"Here is our money," Amy said.

"Let's get something to eat."

And so they did.